# A Bear's Christmas Carol

*A Read-Aloud Adaptation*
*of Charles Dickens'*
*"A Christmas Carol"*

by Vicki J. Kuyper

Illustrations by Laura Ferraro

Current®

To my wonderful family...
God bless them,
each and every one!

— V. J. K.

Book design by Jean McLaren

**A BEAR'S CHRISTMAS CAROL**

Library of Congress Catalog Card Number: 91-75380

ISBN 0-944943-03-9

Once upon a Christmas Eve, in a tiny village
outside London, a crochety, old bear sat counting
his pots of golden honey.

On this night, the most magical of the year, it seemed that every bear in town was preparing for the wonderful celebration to come. Every bear, that is, except Ebearnezer Scrooge...

"I suppose you'll be wanting the entire day off tomorrow?" Scrooge snarled at his clerk. "And expect me to pay you for it as well!"

Bob Scratchit cleared his throat, then answered quietly, "But sir, it's Christmas. It does come only once a year..."

"Bah, humbear!" Scrooge sputtered. "The likes of you will rob me blind! Go ahead. Take your day. But don't think you can hibernate past the first day of spring and find a job waiting for you here!"

"Oh, thank you, sir," Scratchit replied. "Thank you so kindly." Scratchit grabbed his threadbare coat and made his way toward the door of the counting-house with hurried steps, just in case Scrooge changed his mind.

"And a Merry Christmas to you, sir!" Scratchit called back as he closed the door and happily headed for home.

"Merry Christmas, indeed!" Scrooge growled. "Bah, humbear! What a foolish waste of time and honey."

How Scrooge hated Christmas! Tomorrow the entire village would waste every drop of honey they had worked for all year to make cookies, candies, and honey-filled cakes. Then, after a day of feasting and singing, they would all curl up under their warmest quilts and fall into a deep, winter sleep.

All this joy, celebration, and "goodwill toward bears" was more than Scrooge could stand. *He* was a practical bear, one who *knew* the value of a pot of honey. *He* was not about to waste any of *his* sticky, gold fortune on foolishness.

Grumbling, Scrooge locked the counting-house with his pots of honey safely inside. As he turned to leave, he glanced at the sign above the front door. "Scrooge and Snarley," it read. It had been seven years since his partner, Jacob Snarley, had died. Seven years ago that very night...

"Humph," Scrooge muttered to himself, "better have that sign repainted first thing next spring."

Scrooge pulled his coat a little tighter over his graying fur and headed home. Fog as thick as Christmas pudding covered the village. But the bears crowding the cobblestone streets didn't seem to mind the cold. Happy "hellos" and Christmas carols filled the misty evening air. With a snarl on his face, Scrooge quickened his step. He couldn't wait to lock the sights and sounds of Christmas outside his own front door.

"A nice warm bowl of soup by the fire with no one to bother me will be just the thing," Scrooge thought as he walked up his front steps. But as he put his key into the lock, he began to tremble.

There, where the door knocker had always been, was the face of his former partner, Jacob Snarley. Snarley looked as unpleasant there as he had in life, with cold, angry eyes and a tight-lipped sneer. Yet, there was a strange sadness in Snarley's face that made Scrooge's fur stand on end.

Almost as soon as Scrooge began to believe the fog and darkness were *not* playing tricks on him — that Snarley had really come back from the dead — the face disappeared, leaving an ordinary door knocker in its place.

Shaken, but now certain he had only been frightened by a shadow, Scrooge turned the key and went inside.

"Nonsense and poppycock!" Scrooge's voice echoed through the house's empty hallway. Even so, Scrooge lit a candle and inspected the back of the door, just to make sure Snarley's tail wasn't sticking out of it.

Relieved, Scrooge put on his nightshirt and cap, then warmed his soup over the fire. Just as he settled down in his favorite chair, the bells of the town church began to chime.

"Nine bells," mumbled Scrooge to himself. "Goodness! How quickly this evening has flown. It's almost bedtime!"

Mysteriously, the chimes continued to twelve, thirteen, fourteen, and beyond. But, Scrooge was no longer counting the tolling bells. He was staring at the bear now sitting in the chair across from him.

Scrooge closed his eyes, gave them a good rub and opened them again. But the figure was still there.

"You do not believe in me, do you Ebearnezer?" asked the spirit.

"I don't know what to believe," Scrooge replied, trembling. "If it is you, Snarley, you have been dead seven years!"

"I've come to bring you a warning," said the spirit. "Do not end up like me, Ebearnezer, wandering the earth forever, regretting the things you did not do. You still have a chance to change!

"You will be visited by three spirits," Snarley continued. "The first will arrive tonight at one o'clock..."

Then, as suddenly as he had appeared, Snarley was gone.

"Humbear," Scrooge mumbled, but in his heart, he was not so sure. He quickly went upstairs and hid under his quilt, then fell into a deep sleep.

Scrooge awoke with a start at the stroke of
midnight. Moonlight had broken through the fog
and the curtains surrounding his bed glowed with
a peaceful light.

"All a dream," Scrooge reassured himself. "The
whole evening must have been a dream. Imagine!
Snarley alive and talking about visiting spirits…
Bah, humbear!"

But try as he might, Scrooge could not fall
back asleep. He even tried counting pots of
honey, but nothing calmed his nerves. By the
time the bell tolled one, Scrooge was sure the
pounding of his heart must be loud enough to
wake the entire village.

Then he saw it — a small, brown paw drawing back his bed curtains. Scrooge held his breath in fear. But the open curtains revealed only a tiny cub in a white robe, with a belt of holly wrapped around its waist.

"I am the Bear of Christmas Past," the cub said in a gentle, childlike voice.

"Long past?" asked Scrooge.

"No, your past," said the cub. "Come with me."

He led Scrooge toward the open bedroom window. Although Scrooge's heart was still pounding wildly, something about the young bear comforted him. Scrooge willingly took hold of his paw as out the window they flew.

In a twinkling they found themselves in an old warehouse crowded with bears dressed in holiday finery. The aromas of roasting chestnuts, hot cider, and fresh honey cakes filled the air as dancers bounded across the room to the happy sounds of a fiddle. Off to one side, Scrooge saw a plump, grey-haired bear laughing with a young cub.

"Why it's old Fuzzywig! How good to see him again!" said Scrooge. Fascinated, he eavesdropped on their conversation.

"Well, Ebearnezer," the grey-haired bear said to the cub, "I think this is the best party yet!"

"You're right, sir. You've outdone yourself!" grinned the young Scrooge. "I'm sure everyone here would agree that working for you makes every day feel like a holiday!"

"What good is honey if it can't be shared with friends?" Fuzzywig said with a wink.

The spirit turned to a frowning Scrooge. "Is something wrong?" he asked.

"Oh, it's nothing," said Scrooge. "I was just thinking of something I wish I had said to my clerk."

Suddenly, the music stopped and the warehouse disappeared. Scrooge found himself in a meadow of wildflowers, gazing at someone he once thought he would spend his whole life with.

Scrooge had forgotten just how beautiful Honeybell was. He felt happy and sad at the same time as he and the spirit watched Honeybell speaking to the young Scrooge.

"You're not the same bear you were a year ago," Honeybell said quietly.

"I am a better bear!" said Scrooge. "Quitting Fuzzywig's and going out on my own was the best thing I could have done! Soon I will have enough honey to give you anything you want."

"But all I want is the old you," Honeybell wept. "The Ebearnezer who didn't care how much honey he had, the Ebearnezer who always had time to listen and laugh with me. Not the Ebearnezer who only cares about making more honey!"

"But, I love you, Honeybell," the young Scrooge insisted. "In the years to come, you'll see how happy you'll be having a house filled with honey."

"I'm sorry, Ebearnezer. I'm afraid you love honey more than you love me. Good-bye..."

As the sound of Honeybell's voice faded from his ears, Scrooge found himself tossing in his bed. Confused and exhausted, he quickly fell back to sleep.

Once again, Scrooge awoke to the sound of
church bells. Though the room was not cold, he
shivered as he waited for a new spirit to pull open
the bed curtains. But the curtains remained
closed, even after the church bells had stopped
ringing.

It was the delightful smell of hot cider and
honey cake that finally drew Scrooge to open
the curtains himself. His room was filled with
a tremendous holiday feast. Next to a large
Christmas tree sat a bear with a wide smile and
a round tummy.

"Welcome!" said the bear, with a hearty laugh. "I am the Bear of Christmas Present. Follow me... we have so much to see!"

Scrooge's bedroom disappeared as he found himself following the spirit through the familiar streets of his village.

"Where is everyone?" Scrooge asked.

"Take a look!" said the spirit, pointing to a nearby window.

Inside, the house was bursting with excitement. There was a flurry of wrapping paper as five young cubs opened presents around a twinkling tree. Other windows revealed bears praying over their holiday feasts, families singing carols, or cubs merrily playing with new toys.

After they had walked quite far, Scrooge realized he was entering a part of town he rarely saw. The houses were small and run down. Few windows revealed Christmas trees or gaily wrapped gifts. Yet the celebrations taking place in each tiny home held as much love as those filled with mountains of packages.

"A toast to Mr. Scrooge!" came a voice through a crack in a nearby window.

Scrooge tiptoed over and peered inside. Bob Scratchit was making a toast with a small tin cup. Behind him was a dying fire. Scratchit's wife and a roomful of tiny cubs huddled nearby.

"Mr. Scrooge, indeed," said his wife with a growl. "Why should we be thankful for a bear without a heart?"

"I think he's a sad bear, Mama," said a small cub, seated by the fireplace. The cub then pulled himself up on his homemade crutches and hobbled to his father's side.

"I think you're right, Tiny Teddy," said Bob. He gently picked up his son and set him high on his shoulders. "I'd much rather have a home filled with love than all the honey in the world...all the honey in the world...all the honey in the world..."

When Scrooge awoke, still groggy with sleep, he realized that Scratchit's words had changed into the sound of tolling church bells. As he opened his eyes, he saw a figure in a hooded cape standing in the shadows beyond his partially opened bed curtains.

"Are you the Spirit of Christmas Yet to Come?" Scrooge asked, now fully awake. "Are you here to show me my future?"

The figure did not reply. It approached Scrooge in silence and wrapped the dark folds of its cape around him. Everything went black.

Scrooge heard laughter and whispered voices in the darkness. Slowly, his eyes made out the shapes of several ragged bears, huddled together in a dingy alley. They were pawing through pillowcases filled with candlesticks, silverware, and other household trinkets.

"We've certainly hit the honeypot with this load!" one bear growled to another. "Good riddance to the old bear, I say. Look what I pulled right off of his bed before they took him away!"

Scrooge gasped in horror. "Spirit, those are my bed curtains!"

The spirit said nothing, but wrapped his cloak around Scrooge. Everything turned to darkness once more.

23

In an instant, Scrooge was back at the home of the Scratchits. The family was gathered together, just as before, ready for a holiday toast. But, Scrooge was paying little attention to the scene before him. He was uneasy about what he had seen and heard in the murky alleyway. How had his bed curtains made their way into the paws of thieves? And why was he taken away, and to where? Upon hearing his own name, Ebearnezer's thoughts were drawn back to the family gathered before him.

"To Mr. Scrooge," sighed Scratchit.

"I can't stand to hear it anymore," said Mrs. Scratchit. "He never did one thing for anyone but himself. The world is a better place without him!"

"Hush, Martha," said Bob. "It is a sad day when no one cares about the passing of a fellow bear. As Tiny Teddy always used to say, 'God bless us, each and every one...'" Scratchit tried to continue, but his voice broke into muffled sobs.

Martha and all the little Scratchits hurried to his side, comforting him with bear hugs and "I love you's." That is when Scrooge noticed the pair of crutches leaning against the hearth.

"Tell me it's not true!" Scrooge pleaded,
pulling frantically at the spirit's cape. "Please, tell
me there is hope, that the future can be changed!
Oh, Spirit, I beg you, please spare Tiny Teddy! I
give you my word. I will not forget what I have
seen tonight. I promise the spirit of Christmas will
live in my heart every day of the year!"

The spirit said nothing, but wrapped its cloak tightly around Scrooge. But this time, instead of darkness, Scrooge was surrounded by a bright light.

He awoke to find himself wrapped tightly in his bed linens, pleading into his pillow. The church bells were tolling seven as the bright light of day streamed into his room.

"My bed curtains! My wonderful bed curtains are right here where they belong," said Scrooge with a jolly laugh. He flung them wide open and bounded to his window.

The streets below were deserted, except for one small cub in his Sunday best carrying a small pot of honey tied with a big bow. Scrooge threw open the window and called to the young bear. "Hello, lad! Could you be so kind as to tell me what day it is?"

The cub stopped in his tracks and looked around, unsure of where the ridiculous question had come from.

"Over here, boy!" Scrooge yelled again. "Could you kindly tell me what day it is?"

"Why, Christmas day, of course!" said the cub, with a quizzical smile on his face.

"Oh, thank you, sweet spirits! You've finished all in one night!" Scrooge shouted to the early morning sky.

By now, the young cub was convinced that the strange bear hanging out the window in his night-shirt would be best left alone.

"Wait!" Scrooge yelled, as the cub turned to hurry off. "Tell me, does the bakery down the street still have that tremendous honey cake in the window?"

"You mean the one that's as big as I am?" the cub replied. "Sure!"

"Go wake the baker and tell him I want that cake delivered to the home of Bob Scratchit," said Scrooge, laughing merrily. The cub looked up at Scrooge in disbelief.

"Come here and I'll give you a pot of honey for your troubles," yelled Scrooge.

The cub hesitated only a second before running to Scrooge's door. As the excited cub continued on to the bakery, Scrooge donned his holiday best for the first time in years. Grabbing a large pot of honey, Scrooge turned to lock the door of his house.

"Wonderful door knocker!" Scrooge said, patting the plain brass knocker, which the night before had made him shiver with fear. "Thank you for everything!"

Scrooge nearly skipped down the street, pausing to bid a warm "Merry Christmas" to every bear he passed.

Scrooge arrived at the Scratchits at the same time as the honey cake. Both were greeted with great fanfare. Though amazed at Scrooge's sudden change of heart, the Scratchits treated Ebearnezer as one of the family. They shared a day of feasting and laughter and afterward agreed that this Christmas was the best any of them could recall.

When the time came to prepare for their winter naps, Scrooge brought the whole family back to his own home. They curled up together on a cloud of quilts and overstuffed pillows Scrooge had set by a crackling fire.

As Scrooge tucked himself in that wonderful night, he couldn't resist giving one last shout of "Merry Christmas to all!"

And Tiny Teddy replied with a sleepy smile, "And God bless us, each and every one!"

31

The End